CW00865254

With thanks to Val McGouran and all who helped at the Queen Elizabeth Hospital

Blackie Children's Books

Published by the Penguin Group
Penguin Books Ltd. 27 Wrights Lane, London W8 5TZ, England
Penguin Books USA Inc., 375 Hudson Street, New York, New York 10014, USA
Penguin Books Australia Ltd, Ringwood, Victoria, Australia
Penguin Books Canada Ltd, 10 Alcorn Avenue, Toronto, Ontario, Canada M4V 3B2
Penguin Books (NZ) Ltd, 182-190 Wairau Road, Auckland 10, New Zealand

Penguin Books Ltd, Registered Offices: Harmondsworth, Middlesex, England

First published 1993
10 9 8 7 6 5 4 3 2 1

First Edition
Copyright © 1993 Annie West

This edition by arrangement with Libba Jones Associates

The moral right of the author has been asserted

A CIP catalogue record for this book is available from the British Library

ISBN 0 216 94006 0

Printed in Hong Kong

BRINKWORTH BEAR
GOES TO HOSPITAL

ANNIE WEST

Blackie Children's Books

Bertie and Ed were climbing a tree.

Suddenly,a branch broke; Bertie fell with a thud and hurt his knee.

It hurt so much Bertie cried and cried,
He couldn't even walk when he tried.
Bertie's mum phoned the ambulance crew:
When the crew arrived, they knew just what to do.

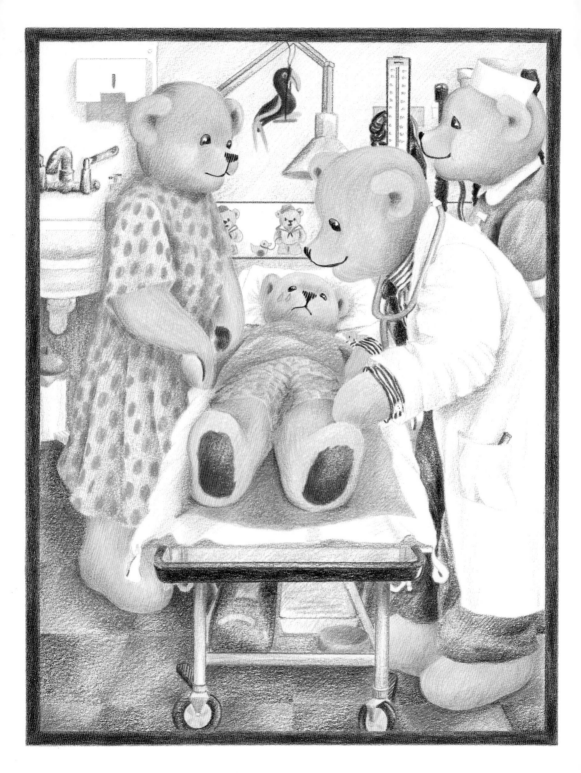

At the hospital a doctor examined Bertie. He was gentle and kind.

He felt all round Bertie's knee to see what he could find.

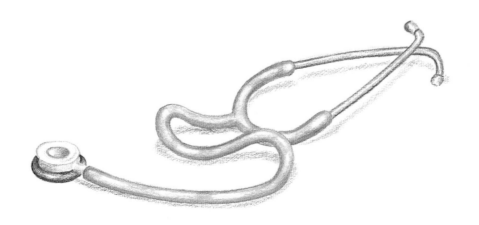

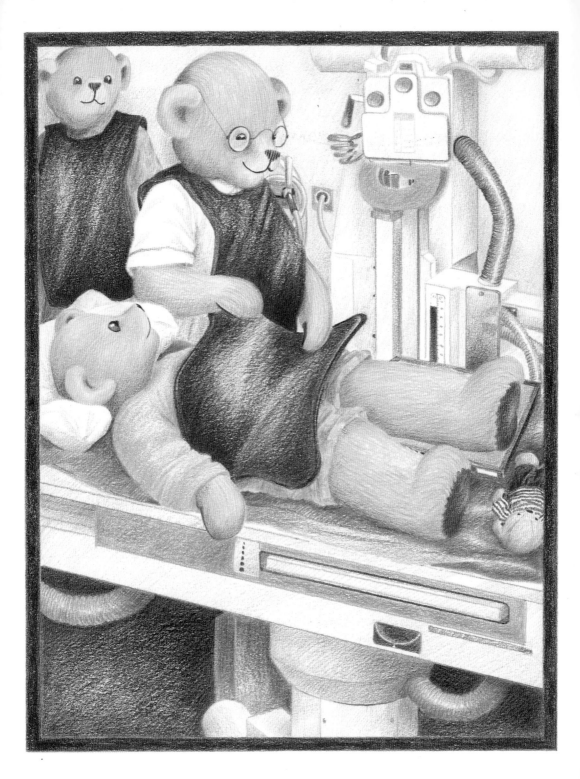

The doctor took an X-ray to be absolutely certain.

A big camera looked right through Bertie's leg, but it didn't hurt him.

From the X-ray picture, the doctor could see

That Bertie's leg was broken just below the knee.

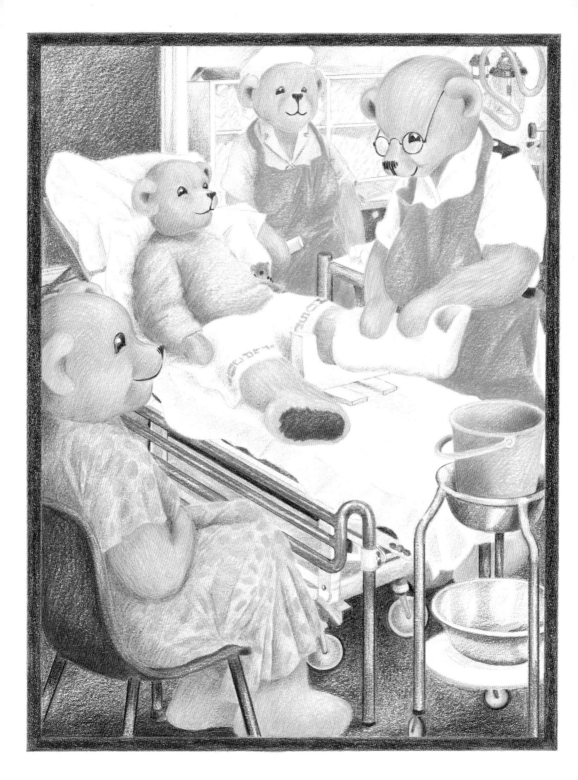

The nurse put layers of bandages and plaster on Bertie's leg. She worked very fast.

Bertie's leg felt quite heavy when it was all finished at last.

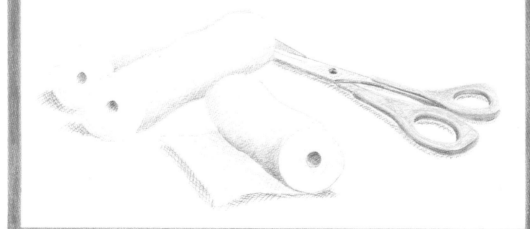

When Bertie's plaster was nearly dry, he carefully wrote his name.

He couldn't wait to get back home and ask his friends to do the same!

When it was time to
go home, the nurses
gave Bertie a badge
for being a brave bear.
Then Bertie and his
mum and dad said
good-bye and thanked
everyone there.